THE CHILDREN'S ILLUSTRATED TREASURY
OF
CLASSIC
FAIRYTALE STORIES

hinkler

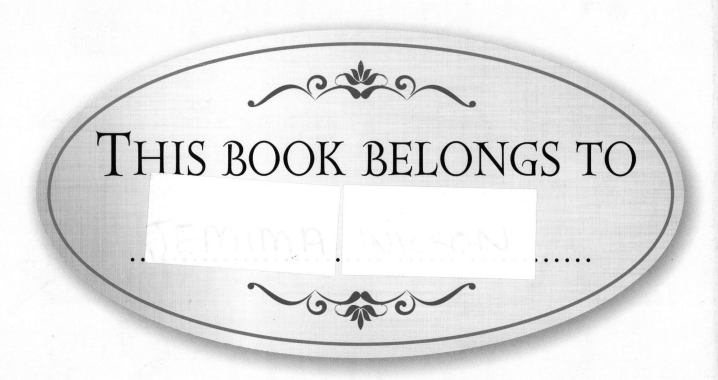

THIS BOOK BELONGS TO

JEMIMA NIXON

THE CHILDREN'S ILLUSTRATED TREASURY

OF

CLASSIC FAIRYTALE STORIES

Published by Hinkler Books Pty Ltd
45–55 Fairchild Street
Heatherton Victoria 3202 Australia
www.hinkler.com.au

hinkler

© Hinkler Books Pty Ltd 2009, 2015

Editor: Louise Coulthard
Cover design: Sam Grimmer
Internal design: Trudi Webb
Illustrators: Melissa Webb, Anton Petrov, Omar Aranda,
Suzie Byrne, Stevie Mahardhika,Mirela Tufan and Brijbasi
Prepress: Graphic Print Group

Images © Hinkler Books Pty Ltd or Shutterstock.com

ISBN 978 1 7428 1971 6

Printed and bound in China

CONTENTS

INTRODUCTION

The tradition of fairytales and folklore is one that has been with us for centuries. Fairytales are found in every culture and often surprisingly similar stories will have developed on different sides of the world. Regardless of their origins, fairytales can be happy or sad; frightening or reassuring; dark or light; or all of these at once.

The common thing that binds all fairytales together is that they are about the emotions, fears, joys, hopes and dreams that we all share. Whether the fears are expressed through an encounter with a fearsome witch or the joys are found in a princess re-awakened, fairytales touch on feelings and experiences that we can all relate to. Everyone is searching for their very own 'happily ever after'.

This collection brings together some classic tales from a range of fairytale traditions, be it the scholarly works of the German Brothers Grimm, the tradition of British folk stories, the imagination of Dane Hans Christian Andersen or the courtly tales of Frenchman Charles Perrault. Whatever the source, these fairytales are a much-loved part of growing up and learning about the joys and perils of the world.

Everyone has their own version of their favourite tales. The stories in this collection have tried to stay as close to the original versions as possible, but everyone has a different way of telling them. We hope you enjoy our versions. Share them as a family and discover the joys and rewards of reading together.

SLEEPING BEAUTY

Once upon a time in a faraway country there lived a king and queen. They lived in a beautiful castle and had many fine clothes, jewels and treasures. Although they had been married for many years, they were very sad, as they had no children.

One day, the queen was walking beside the river at the bottom of the garden. Suddenly, she saw a little fish that had thrown itself on the shore, gasping for air. Filled with pity, she picked it up and placed it back into the river. Before it swam away, the fish lifted its head out of the water and said, 'I know what you wish for and it shall come true. You will soon have a daughter.'

What the fish had foretold came to pass and the queen had a little girl. The king was overjoyed and announced a great feast to celebrate. He invited all his friends and kinsmen, as well as all the nobles and members of the court.

As was the tradition, the queen invited the fairies so that they might bestow gifts on the new princess. There were eight fairies in the kingdom but the king and queen only had seven gold dishes for the fairies to eat from, so they were forced to leave one out.

At the end of the feast, the fairies presented the princess with their gifts. The first fairy said the princess would be the most beautiful girl in the world. The second fairy gave her wit and intelligence and the third bestowed gracefulness on her. The fourth said she should dance perfectly, the fifth that she would sing beautifully and the sixth that she would play all kinds of music flawlessly.

Suddenly, in a flash of lightning, the eighth fairy appeared. She was very angry that she had not been invited to the feast. Determined to have her revenge, she cried out, 'Here is my gift! In her sixteenth year, the king's daughter shall prick her finger with a spindle and fall down dead!'

The king and queen were horrified, but the seventh fairy stepped forward. 'I have not yet given my gift,' she said. 'This evil wish must be fulfilled but I can soften it. The princess will not die when the spindle wounds her but she will fall asleep. After one hundred years, the son of a king shall wake her.'

The king, hoping to save his daughter, issued a decree that all spindles should be immediately destroyed and banned them from his entire kingdom. As the princess grew up, the gifts of the first six fairies all came true. The princess was beautiful, good and wise and everyone who knew her loved her.

One day, when the princess was in her sixteenth year, the king and queen went away on a royal visit, leaving the princess behind in the castle. She roved around the castle, exploring every room, tower and apartment. Finally, she came to a little room at the top of a tower, where she found a good old woman sitting at a spinning wheel with her spindle.

'Good mother, what are you doing there?' asked the princess. She had never seen a spinning wheel before because they had all been destroyed.

'I am spinning flax, my child,' said the old lady.

'How prettily the wheel spins around!' exclaimed the princess. 'May I have a try?'

But no sooner did the princess pick up the spindle than she pricked herself with it and fell down in a deep sleep. The old lady cried out for help and people came rushing from all quarters. They shook the princess, they threw cold water upon her face, they tried everything they could to wake her but still she slumbered.

The king and queen rushed home to their daughter's side. Remembering the fairy's prediction, they ordered that the princess be laid out in the finest apartment in the palace on a bed embroidered with gold and silver thread. Despairing of ever seeing her awake again, the king sorrowfully commanded that all should leave the princess and let her sleep in peace.

Now the good fairy who had saved the princess's life was far away in another country, but when she heard the news, she set off at once to the palace in a chariot of fire drawn by dragons. The king met her and helped her down from the chariot. The fairy approved of all the arrangements but realised that if the poor princess slept for one hundred years, she would wake up orphaned and alone, surrounded by strangers.

So the good fairy touched everything in the palace with her wand: the king and queen; the ministers of state; the members of the court; the maids of honour and the gentlemen in waiting; the bishops and the clergy; the governesses and the professors; the guards and the footmen; the pages and the heralds; the stewards and the cooks; and even the horses in the stables, the dogs in the yard and the princess's little pet puppy.

As soon as the fairy's wand touched them, everyone fell asleep, ready to wake with the princess. The spits in the kitchen stopped turning and the clocks stopped ticking and the whole castle slept. Then the fairy caused a great forest of thick trees, brambles and thorns to grow up around the castle so that only the very top of the towers could be seen and no one could come near. The castle lay quiet and undisturbed for years and years and eventually everyone forgot that it existed and who had lived there.

When a hundred years had passed, a prince was out hunting nearby. During the chase, he saw the thick wood and asked, 'What is this wood and what are those towers I can see appearing in the midst of it?'

No one could answer him. Some said that it was an old ruin, haunted by ghosts. Others said that a great ogre lived there and still others that it was the home of a band of evil witches.

Finally, an old woodcutter told the prince of a tale that he had heard from his grandfather. 'If it may please Your Highness,' said the old woodcutter, 'my grandfather used to say that in the forest is an enchanted castle. In this castle sleeps a beautiful princess, waiting for a prince to wake her.'

Hearing this, the prince was determined to explore the castle. He pushed his way through the trees and brambles of the thick forest. To his surprise, the bushes parted easily and the prince was able to make his way through, but when his men tried to follow, the trees closed in behind him, blocking their way.

Finally, the thick forest gave way and the prince found himself at the gates of a huge castle. He walked through the massive front gate and entered a wide open yard, where he was first struck with fear. Littered around the courtyard were the bodies of men and horses. However, looking closer, he saw that their faces were rosy and pink and their chests rose and fell as they slumbered.

Continuing on, the prince entered a court paved with marble, where he found rows of guards standing at attention, all asleep. He entered the throne room and saw the king and queen asleep on their thrones. The ministers of state were slumbering at their desks, pens in hand. All their clothes were as fresh as the day they had been washed and there was no dust or cobwebs to be seen.

As he wandered, the prince found rooms filled with lords and ladies, some standing, some sitting, but all asleep. Seamstresses were asleep over their sewing, cooks were sleeping over their pots and maids slumbered leaning on their brooms. He came to a grand staircase and made his way up, where he found apartments and rooms filled with sleeping people.

Finally, he came to the most grand apartment of all. Opening the door, he entered a room and found a bed beautifully embroidered with gold and silver thread. Lying on it was the most beautiful girl he'd ever seen. Her face was fresh and rosy, as though she had only just fallen asleep.

Trembling, the prince approached the bed and knelt beside her. He gazed at her lovely face a while, then lifted her white hand to his lips and gently kissed it.

At this, the long enchantment was broken. The princess opened her eyes and smiled at him. 'You have been a long while coming, my prince,' she said. The prince was charmed by these words and swore he loved her more than anything. The happy couple talked together for many hours, although the prince did not tell her that her dress was one hundred years out of fashion.

Meanwhile, the rest of the castle awakened. The prince and princess made their way down the great stairs, where the princess was happily reunited with her parents. A great feast was proclaimed, as everyone who had not just fallen in love was very hungry.

The great forest surrounding the castle disappeared as soon as the princess woke up. The whole country celebrated as the prince and princess were married in the castle. The good fairy blessed them and they lived happily ever after.

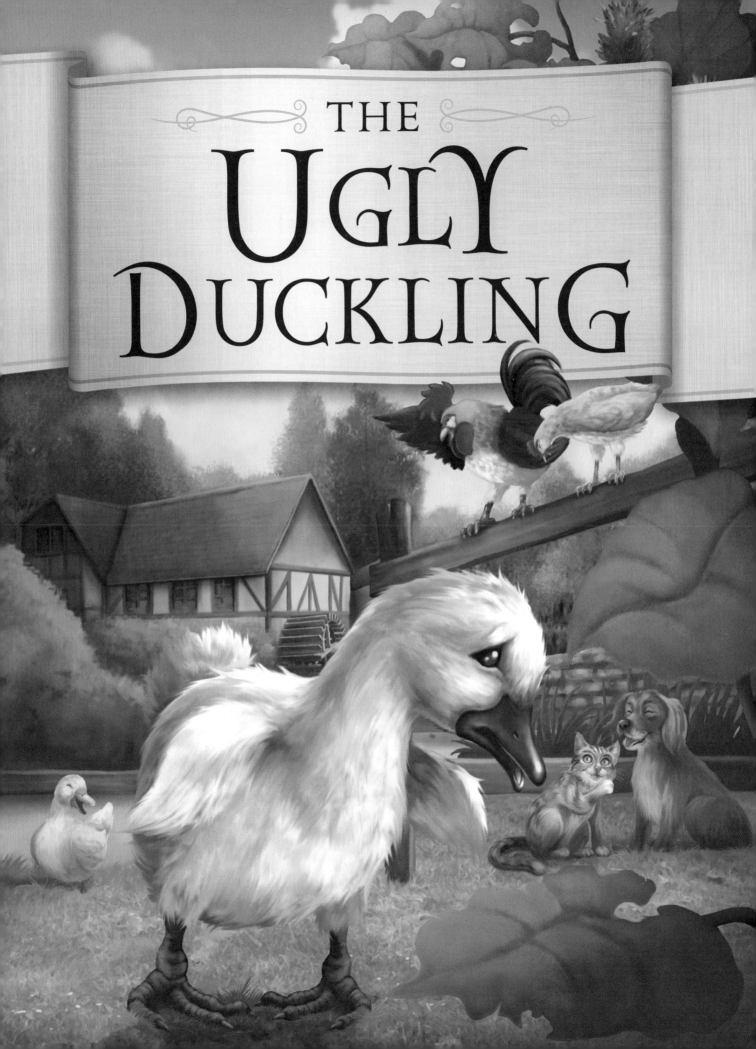

THE UGLY DUCKLING

It was a beautiful summer in the countryside. The corn was golden, the oats were green and the haystacks were piled up in the meadows. The stork walked about on his long red legs chattering away in Egyptian, which his mother had taught him. Surrounding the cornfields and meadows were large forests, in the midst of which were deep lakes. It was indeed lovely.

In a sunny spot near a deep river stood a pleasant old farmhouse. Along the river grew great burdock leaves, so tall that a child could stand underneath them.

In this snug spot, a duck sat on her nest, waiting for her eggs to hatch. She was beginning to get tired of waiting, as her little ones were a long time coming out of their shells and she didn't get many visitors. The other ducks much preferred to swim in the cool river than to climb the muddy slope and gossip with her.

At last, the egg shells cracked, one after the other. From each egg came a little creature that raised its head and cried out, 'Peep, peep!'

'Quack, quack,' said the mother, and then they all quacked as well as they could and looked about them at the large green leaves. Their mother let them look as much as they liked, for green is good for the eyes.

'Are you all hatched?' asked the duck. 'No, I do declare, the biggest egg is still here. I hope this doesn't last too long, as I am quite tired of it.' She settled herself back down on the nest.

An old duck came to visit. 'How are you getting on?' she asked.

'One egg is still not hatched,' replied the duck. 'But the others are the prettiest ducklings you'll ever see!'

The old duck looked at the large unhatched egg. 'I am sure that is a turkey's egg. I was tricked into hatching some once. After all my trouble, they were afraid to go into the water. Take my advice. Leave it where it is and teach the other children to swim.'

'I will sit on it for a little longer,' said the duck. 'A few days longer will be nothing.'

'As you wish,' said the old duck, and she took her leave.

At last, the large egg hatched. A young bird crept out, crying 'Peep, peep!' It was very large and ugly with grey feathers. The duck exclaimed, 'It is so large and not at all like the others! Maybe it really is a turkey. I'll find out when we go to the water. It will go in, even if I have to push it in.'

The next day, the sun shone brightly on the green burdock leaves, so the mother duck took her children down to the water. She jumped in and cried 'Quack, quack!' One after the other, the ducklings tumbled in after her. The water closed over their heads but they all popped up in an instant and were soon swimming about prettily with their legs paddling away underneath them. The ugly duckling was also in the water, swimming as well as any of them.

'Well, he is not a turkey,' said the mother. 'See how well he paddles and how he holds himself upright. He is not so ugly if you look at him properly. Come now children, I will take you into society and introduce you to the farmyard. Stay close to me so you are not stepped on, and, above all, look out for the cat!'

When they reached the farmyard, the mother duck said, 'Let me see how well you can behave. Bow your heads to that old duck there. She is the highest born of them all. See how she has a red flag tied to her leg? It is a great honour and shows that everyone is anxious not to lose her. Come now, bend your neck and say "quack".'

The ducklings did as they were told, but the other ducks stared and said, 'What a queer-looking duckling one of them is!' One spiteful duck flew at the ugly duckling and bit him.

'Leave him alone!' cried his mother. 'He is not doing any harm.'

'He is so big and ugly,' said the nasty duck, 'and he should be turned away.'

'The others are very pretty,' said the old duck. 'What a shame this one cannot be hatched again!'

'He is not very pretty, your ladyship,' said the mother duck, 'but he has a very good disposition and swims better than the others. I think he has just stayed in the egg too long and his figure is not properly formed.'

'The other ducklings are graceful enough,' said the old duck. 'Now make yourself at home.'

The family made themselves at home. But the ugly duckling was chased and pushed and bitten and jeered at by all the poultry in the farmyard. It grew worse every day. The poor duckling was hunted by everyone and even his brothers and sisters taunted him and his mother said she wished he had never been born. At last, he ran away, frightening the little birds in the hedge as he flew over.

'They are afraid because I am so ugly,' the ugly duckling thought. He closed his eyes and flew until he came to a large moor where some wild ducks lived. Here he stayed the night, very tired and sorrowful.

In the morning, the wild ducks stared at him. 'What sort of duck are you?' they asked, crowding around. The duckling bowed to them but he didn't answer.

'You are very ugly,' the wild ducks said, 'but you seem nice and you can stay as long as you don't want to marry any of us.' Poor duckling! All he wanted was to lie among the rushes and drink some water.

He had been there two days when two young wild geese, or rather goslings, came to him. 'You are so ugly that we like you well,' one said. 'Will you travel with us?'

'Pop, pop!' suddenly sounded in the air, and the two geese fell down dead. 'Pop, pop' echoed out and the ducks and geese rose up into the air. Hunters had surrounded the moor and the sound continued from every direction. Then the hunting dogs came running through the rushes.

The poor duckling was terrified! A large, terrible dog came bounding past him with its jaws wide open and its tongue hanging out. It sniffed at the ugly duckling and bared its teeth and its wild eyes gleamed, and then it splashed away without touching him. 'I am so ugly that not even a dog would bite me,' sighed the duckling.

All day he lay still while the guns boomed overhead. It wasn't until late in the day that it became quiet, but the ugly duckling was too scared to move for several hours. He ran away from the moor as fast as he could until a storm blew up.

As night fell, he came to a poor little cottage. The storm was so wild that the duckling could struggle on no further and he sat down beside it. He noticed that one of the door's hinges had given out and the door slanted in such a way that he could sneak inside, which, very quietly, he did.

An old woman lived in the cottage with her tom cat and her prize hen. In the morning, they discovered their guest and the cat began to purr and the hen clucked. 'What is all the noise about?' asked the old woman.

Her eyesight was not very good, so when the old woman saw the duckling, she thought it must be a duck. 'What luck!' she exclaimed. 'Now we shall have duck eggs, unless it is a drake. I'll wait and see.'

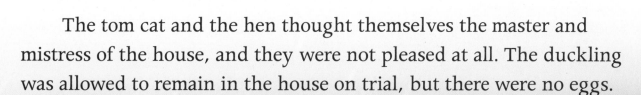

The tom cat and the hen thought themselves the master and mistress of the house, and they were not pleased at all. The duckling was allowed to remain in the house on trial, but there were no eggs.

'Can you lay eggs?' the hen asked the duckling.

'No,' he replied.

'Then hold your tongue!' said the hen.

'Can you arch your back, or purr, or hiss?' asked the cat.

'No,' replied the duckling.

'Then stay quiet when sensible people are talking!' said the cat.

The duckling stayed in the corner, feeling very low and sad. Then one day the sunshine and fresh air came into the room through the open door. The duckling was seized with such a longing to go swimming that he could not help but tell the hen about it.

'What is this nonsense?' cried the hen. 'You have nothing to do, so you are filling your head with fancies. If you could lay eggs or purr, you wouldn't have these ideas.'

'But it is so delightful to swim on the water,' said the duckling, 'and so refreshing to dive down to the bottom.'

'Why, you must be crazy!' said the hen. 'Ask the cat if he would like to swim about on the water. Ask our mistress if she would like to dive down and let the water close over her head! I advise you to learn to purr and lay eggs as soon as possible.'

'You don't understand me,' said the duckling. 'I think I must go out into the world again.'

'Indeed you must,' said the hen, and so the ugly duckling left the cottage. Soon he found some water to swim and dive in, but the other animals avoided him because he was so ugly. Autumn came and the leaves turned gold. As winter approached, the trees grew bare and heavy dark clouds hung in the sky.

One evening, as the sun was setting, a large flock of beautiful birds flew overhead. The duckling had never seen any creatures like them before. They were swans, with dazzling white feathers and long, graceful necks, who were flying to warmer countries. They uttered a peculiar cry as they flew.

The ugly duckling felt quite strange as he watched them. He whirled around in the water and, stretching out his neck towards them, he uttered a cry so strange that it frightened him. He was beside himself with excitement and knew that he would never forget those beautiful, proud birds. He felt towards them as he had never felt towards any other creature.

As winter closed in, the weather grew colder and colder. The ugly duckling had to swim about on the water to stop it from freezing, but every morning the space he had left to swim in grew smaller and smaller.

Finally, the water began to freeze around him and he had to paddle with his legs as hard as he could to stop the space from closing completely. He grew so exhausted that he lay still and helpless, frozen in the ice.

The next morning, a farmer was passing by when he found the duckling. He broke the ice around the duckling with his shoe and carried him home to his wife.

The farmer's wife revived the poor creature and then the farmer's children tried to play with him. Not understanding, the duckling thought they wanted to harm him. In his terror, he fluttered into the milk pan and splashed milk about the room. Then he flew into the butter tub and into the meal barrel and out again. What a state he was in!

The woman yelled and chased him with her broom while the children laughed and screamed and fell over each other as they tried to catch him. At last, he slipped out through the open door and lay down exhausted under a bush in the snow.

The poor duckling endured many miseries and privations during the hard winter. He was surviving out on a moor when the sun began to shine and the birds began to sing again for spring.

The duckling found that his wings were stronger and he rose up into the air. He flew until he found himself in a large garden. The trees were in blossom and a stream wound its way through the grounds. Then the duckling saw three beautiful white swans swimming lightly over the smooth water. He remembered these beautiful birds and felt more unhappy than ever.

'I will go to these birds,' he thought. 'Even if they kill me because I am so ugly and I dare to approach them, it would be better than being pecked by the ducks, beaten by the hens or starving of hunger in the winter.'

The duckling landed on the water and swam towards the swans. When they saw him, they rushed to him with wings outstretched.

'Kill me,' said the poor duckling, and he bowed his head down and waited for them to strike him.

But what did he see reflected in the clear stream? He saw his own image; no longer an ugly, grey duckling but a beautiful, graceful young swan. To be born in a duck's nest is of no consequence if one is born a swan. The duckling felt glad to have suffered all the sorrow and hardship, for he was better able to enjoy the pleasure and happiness he now felt. The other swans swam around him and welcomed him.

Some young children came into the garden and threw some bread into the water. 'There is a new one!' they cried. They ran to their mother and father, shouting, 'There is a new swan arrived! He is the most beautiful of all! He is so young and pretty!' And the older swans bowed their heads to him.

Then he felt ashamed and hid his head under his wing, for he did not know what to do. He was so happy, but he was not at all proud. He had been hated for his ugliness and now he heard them saying he was the most beautiful. The sun shone warm and bright and he lifted his head and cried out joyfully, from the bottom of his heart, 'I never dreamed of such happiness as this, when I was an ugly duckling!'

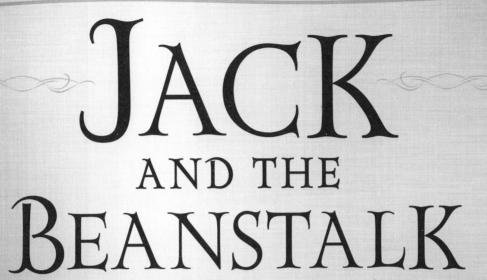

JACK
AND THE
BEANSTALK

Once upon a time there lived a poor widow in a little cottage with her only son Jack. They were very poor. Jack had no work, so all they had to live on was the milk given by their cow, Milky-White, which they took to market each morning and sold. Jack was a kind-hearted and quick boy, but he was also giddy and wilful.

Then one day, Milky-White stopped giving milk. After several days of this, Jack's mother said to him, 'We must sell Milky-White at the market and use the money to start a shop or something.'

'All right Mother,' said Jack. 'Today is market day. I'll soon sell Milky-White and then we'll see what we can do with the money. I'll make sure I get the best price I can.'

So Jack took Milky-White's rope and set off down the road with her to town. As he walked along, he met a funny-looking old man who stopped and said to him, 'Hello Jack! Where are you off to?'

'Good morning,' replied Jack, wondering all the while how this strange fellow knew his name. 'I'm off to market to sell our cow.'

The man stretched out his hand and showed Jack five curious beans. They were all sorts of colours and shimmered and shone. 'These beans are of great value. I'd be prepared to do a swap with you – your cow for my beans.'

'You don't say,' said Jack. He agreed to the sale and handed over Milky-White's rope.

Jack headed home again, the five beans in his pocket. His mother was surprised to see him home so soon.

'Back already Jack?' she asked. 'How much did you sell Milky-White for? What, five pounds? Ten? Fifteen? Surely not twenty!'

'What about these?' said Jack and he stretched out his hands to show her the beans. His mother took them and looked at them.

'What!' she exclaimed. 'Have you been such a fool as to give away my Milky-White for a handful of beans? What shall we do? How could you? As for these beans, out the window they go!'

Jack's angry mother threw the beans out the window and sent him to bed without any supper. He was very sad and sorry, not just for the missed supper but for his mother's sake as well. It was several hours before he fell asleep.

When Jack woke up the next morning, his room seemed
different. Normally bright and sunny, it was strangely dark and
shady. He ran to his window and looked out. To his amazement
he saw that the beans had grown in the night. They had formed
a beanstalk that climbed up and up until it vanished into the
clouds. Jack ran down to the garden to take a closer look.

'Why, those beans have twined together so that you could climb it like a ladder,' thought Jack. 'I wonder where it ends.'

Jack began to climb the beanstalk. It bore his weight easily. He climbed until everything below him – his house, the road, the town – all began to look quite small. He climbed and he climbed and he climbed until he was quite tired. He stopped to rest for a short while, and then he continued on.

Finally, Jack reached the top of the beanstalk. He found himself next to a long straight road that ran through some lovely countryside of woods, pastures and a crystal clear stream burbling along. In the far distance along the road stood a great castle of stone.

Jack set off along the road towards the castle. He walked and walked until he came to the stone castle. Standing on the doorstep was a big tall woman. She was a giant.

'Good morning ma'am,' said Jack politely. 'Would you be so kind as to give me some breakfast?' Jack was as hungry as a hunter, as he was sent to bed without his supper.

'It's breakfast you want, is it?' said the woman. 'It's breakfast you'll be if you don't get along. My man is a giant and there's nothing he likes better than a boy for breakfast! He'll be here soon. Move along or I'll cook you myself!'

'Oh please ma'am, don't cook me,' said Jack. 'I'd be willing to serve you if you'd be so good as to hide me from your husband and give me some breakfast.'

'There's a good boy,' said the giantess, very pleased with the idea of a boy to help her. She took Jack into the kitchen and gave him a hunk of bread and cheese and some milk.

As Jack was finishing his breakfast, the whole house started to shake. Jack heard a loud noise in the distance, getting closer. Thump! Thump! Thump!

'It's my husband!' exclaimed the giantess. 'Quick, hide in here!' She bundled Jack into the oven and shut the door just as the giant came in.

The giant was enormous. He had been out hunting and had three calves hanging from his belt. 'Cook me a couple of these for my breakfast!' he bellowed and flung them on the table. Then the giant paused, sniffed the air and cried out in a voice like thunder:

'Fee-fi-fo-fum,

I smell the blood of an Englishman!

Be he alive or be he dead,

I'll grind his bones to make my bread.'

Then he shouted, 'There is a man in the castle! Let me have him for my breakfast!'

'Nonsense,' said the giantess. 'You've grown old and silly! It must be the man you had for dinner yesterday. Go and wash up and I'll have your breakfast ready for you.'

The giant left to wash up and Jack opened the oven door to jump out, but the giantess told him to wait. 'He will have a sleep after breakfast and then you can come out,' she said.

The giantess cooked two of the calves for the giant's breakfast which he wolfed down hungrily. Then the giant went to a big chest and took out some bags of gold. He sat down and began to count out the money, until eventually his head began to nod and he started to snore so loudly that the house shook.

Jack crept out of the oven. As he went past the giant, he took one of the bags of gold and then ran as fast as he could to the beanstalk. He threw down the gold and climbed down after it. When he got home, he showed his mother the bag of gold and said, 'See mother? Wasn't I right to buy those beans? They are magical!'

Jack and his mother lived off the gold for some time, but at last it ran out. He decided to try his luck at the top of the beanstalk again. Jack climbed and he climbed until he reached the top. When he came to the castle, the giantess was again standing on the doorstep.

'Good morning,' said Jack. 'Could you give me some breakfast?'

The giantess looked at him suspiciously, unsure if she knew him. 'Go away boy,' she said, 'or my husband will eat you for breakfast. But wait, are you the youngster who came here before? My husband lost a bag of gold that day.'

'That's strange ma'am,' said Jack. 'I dare say I could tell you something about that but I'm so hungry that I couldn't speak until I'd had some breakfast.'

The giantess was curious, so she took Jack in and gave him some breakfast. As he was finishing, Jack heard a loud thumping in the distance and the house began to shake. 'Quick, into the oven!' exclaimed the giantess, and Jack scrambled in. The giant bellowed:

'Fee-fi-fo-fum,
I smell the blood of an Englishman!
Be he alive or be he dead,
I'll grind his bones to make my bread.'

The giantess scolded him and the giant had his breakfast. Then he said, 'Wife, bring me my hen that lays the gold eggs.'

The giantess brought in the hen and the giant said, 'Lay!' The hen laid an egg made entirely of gold. After a while, the giant's head began to nod and he started to snore so loudly that the house shook.

Jack crept out of the oven, grabbed hold of the hen and ran for all he was worth. As he ran, the hen cackled and Jack heard the giant wake up and call out, 'Wife, wife, what have you done with the hen?'

That was all Jack heard before he rushed down the beanstalk. When he got home, he showed his mother the hen and said 'Lay' to it. It laid a golden egg every time he told it to.

Still, Jack was not content and decided to try his luck up the beanstalk again. He climbed and he climbed until he reached the top but this time he did not walk along the road to the house.

Jack crept along and hid behind a bush until he saw the giantess come out to the well. Then he slipped into the house and climbed into a large copper boiler. He hadn't been there long before he heard a loud thumping noise and the giant and his wife came into the kitchen.

The giant sniffed and then bellowed:

'Fee-fi-fo-fum,

I smell the blood of an Englishman!

Be he alive or be he dead,

I'll grind his bones to make my bread.'

'Do you?' asked the giantess. 'If it's that little rogue who stole your gold and your hen, he's bound to be in the oven.'

Luckily, Jack had not hidden there, and the giantess said, 'Well, there you go again with your fee-fi-fo-fum! It must be that man we ate last night that you can smell.'

The giant sat down to breakfast, but throughout the meal, he kept muttering 'I could swear…' to himself and he would get up and look in the larder and the cupboards. Luckily, he did not think of the copper boiler. After breakfast, the giant said, 'Wife, bring me my golden harp.'

The giantess put the harp on the table in front of him and the giant said, 'Sing!' At once, the golden harp began to sing most beautifully. It sang until the giant's head began to nod and he started to snore so loudly that the house shook.

Then Jack quietly lifted the lid of the boiler and climbed out. He crept up to the table and grabbed hold of the golden harp and dashed to the door.

But the magic harp called out, 'Master! Master!' in a loud voice, and the giant woke to see Jack running out the door.

Jack ran as fast as he could but the giant ran faster. He had nearly caught Jack when they reached the beanstalk and Jack dodged and then disappeared down into the ground. The giant looked down and saw Jack climbing down for dear life.

For a minute, the giant hesitated and then he swung himself down on to the beanstalk. It swayed and shook with the giant's weight as he made his way down.

Jack climbed faster and faster until he was nearly home. Then he called out, 'Mother! Mother! Bring the axe! Bring the axe!'

Jack's mother came rushing out with the axe in her hand, but stopped in fright when she saw the giant making his way down the beanstalk. Jack jumped down and grabbed the axe and chopped at the mighty beanstalk until it was cut in two.

The beanstalk began to topple and fall, and the terrible giant fell down with it and lay still, never to eat anyone again.

By selling the golden eggs and showing the golden harp, Jack and his mother became very rich. Jack married a great princess and they all lived happily ever after, but they never knew what became of the funny-looking old man who sold Jack the beans.

THE FROG PRINCE

Once upon a time, there lived a king. His daughters were all beautiful, but the youngest was the most beautiful of all. A great forest lay next to the king's castle and in that forest was a deep well. On hot days, the youngest daughter would go to the forest and sit under a tree next to the well to play in the cool shade. The young princess's favourite plaything was a lovely golden ball, and there she would sit, tossing her ball in the air and catching it.

Alas, one day as she was sitting by the well, the princess threw her golden ball so high that instead of falling into her outstretched hand, it bounced away and rolled across the grass into the depths of the well. The princess ran to the side of the well, but she looked for her ball in vain, as the well was so deep that no one could see the bottom. The young princess began to weep at the loss of her favourite toy and could find no comfort.

As she sat crying, the young princess heard someone call out to her. 'Why do you weep so, princess?' said the voice. 'You cry so hard that you would even break the heart of a stone.'

The princess looked up to see where the voice was coming from and saw that a frog had lifted his ugly head out of the well and was talking to her.

'Alas, nasty frog,' she replied, 'I am weeping for my lovely golden ball. It has fallen into the well and is lost. Oh, what I would give to get it back!'

'Do not cry princess,' replied the slimy frog. 'I can help you, but what would you give me if I bring your ball back to you?'

'Whatever you ask for, dear frog,' said the princess. 'I would give all my fine clothes, my jewels, my pearls and even the precious golden crown on my head if I could get my ball back!'

'I care not for fine clothes, jewels, pearls or golden crowns,' answered the frog. 'But if you will love me and let me be your friend and playmate, and sit by you at your little table, and eat off your golden plate and drink out of your golden cup, and sleep on your pillow in your bed – if you will promise me this – then I will bring you back your golden ball from the depths of the well.'

'Oh yes!' cried the princess. 'If you will bring me my ball back, I promise I will do all you ask!'

But the princess was really thinking, 'How silly this frog is! All he can do is sit in the well with the other frogs and croak all day long. He's not fit to be anybody's playmate!'

So the frog dived down deep into the well. After a while, he swam back up to the surface again, holding the princess's golden ball in his mouth. He threw the ball over the edge of the well on to the grass and the princess ran and joyfully picked it up.

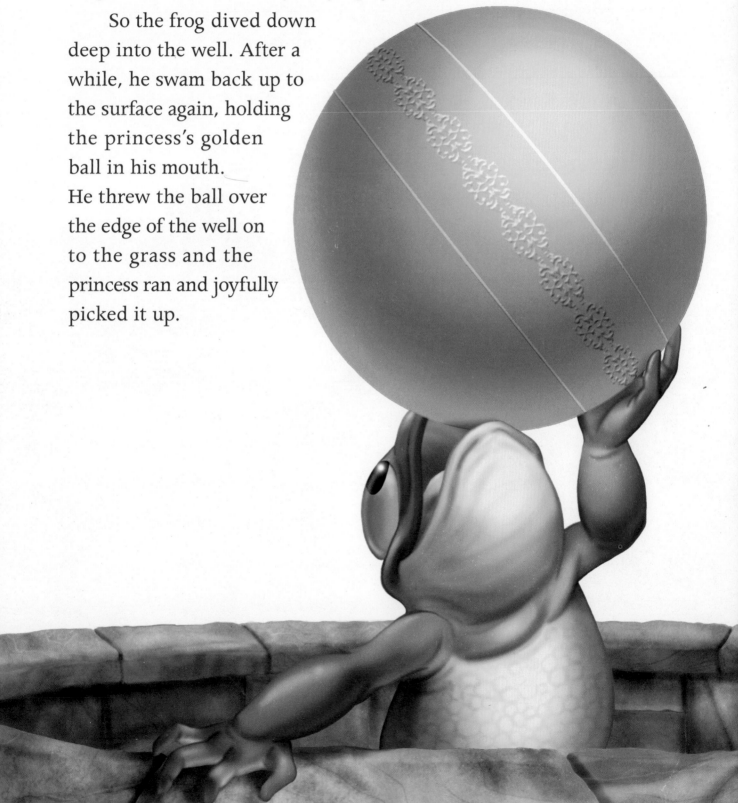

The princess was so happy to have her ball back that she ran away merrily, giving no thought to the frog and her promise.

'Wait princess! Don't forget your promise!' cried the frog. 'Take me with you! I cannot run as fast as you!'

But the princess did not hear the cries of the frog as she ran home to the castle. The poor frog was left to dive sadly back into the well.

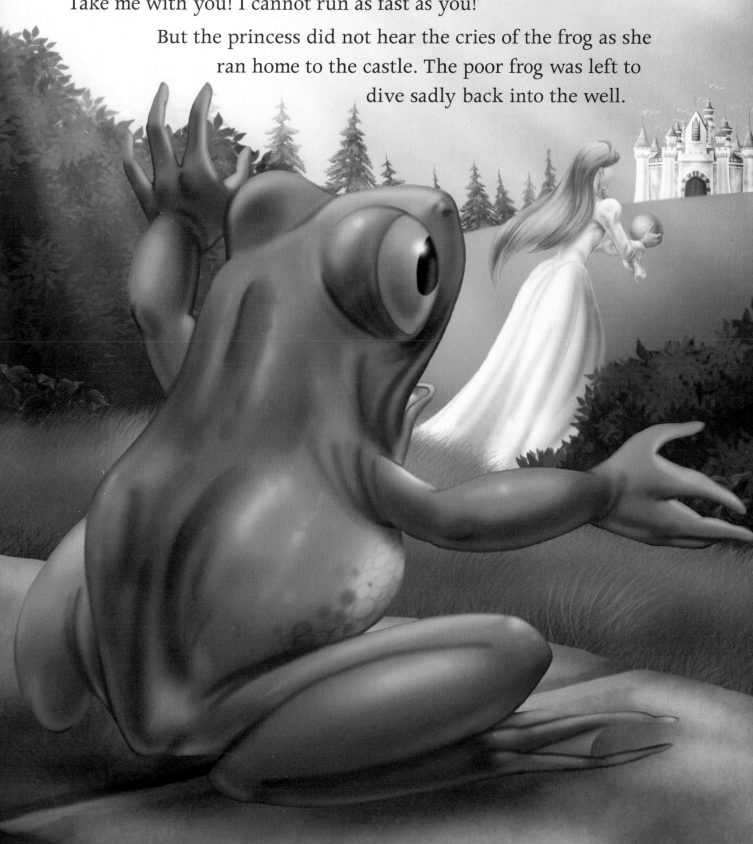

The next day, the young princess was sitting at dinner with her father and her sisters, eating from her golden plate and drinking from her golden cup. All of a sudden, she heard a strange noise that sounded like something coming up the marble staircase: splish, splash, splish, splash. Soon there was a gentle knock at the door and then a voice cried out:

'Open the door, youngest daughter,
Remember thy promise, by the water!
Open the door, princess dear!
Thy true love, awaits thee here!'

The princess ran to the door to see who was there, but when she opened it, she saw the frog from the well sitting there. She slammed the door in fright and ran back to the table.

However, her father saw that something had frightened her and so he asked her, 'What ails you my daughter? Has some beast come to carry you away?'

'It is no beast, father,' the young princess explained. 'It is nothing but an ugly frog.'

'A frog?' asked the surprised king. 'What does a frog want with you?'

'Yesterday I was playing with my golden ball near the well,' the princess replied. 'It fell in the water and I couldn't get it out because the well is so deep. However, this frog fetched it for me after I promised that he could be my companion. I never thought he would leave the well, but here he is at the door, knocking to come in.'

Again there was a knock at the door, and again the frog cried out:

'Open the door, youngest daughter,

Remember thy promise, by the water!

Open the door, princess dear!

Thy true love, awaits thee here!'

The king turned to his daughter and said, 'As you have given your promise, you must keep your word. Do not refuse to help someone who has helped you. Go and let the frog in.'

So the princess opened the door and let the frog in. He hopped along behind her, following her back to her place at the table.

'Lift me up so I may eat off your golden plate and drink out of your golden cup!' the frog cried.

The princess tried to resist, but her father commanded her to keep her promise. 'You must keep your promise, daughter,' said the king.

So the princess lifted the frog up on to the table, where he ate from her golden plate and sipped from her golden cup. The frog ate well, but the princess hardly touched a morsel, so disgusted and upset was she.

Then the frog said, 'Now princess, I am tired. Carry me upstairs to your room and let me sleep next to you in your bed.'

The princess began to cry, as she hated the thought of the nasty frog asleep in her pretty silk sheets, but her father looked at her angrily and again said, 'As you have given your promise, you must keep your word. Do not forget your pledge. Remember, he helped you when you were in trouble.'

So the young princess carried the frog upstairs to her bedroom and laid him on her pillow, where he slept all night. As soon as the sun rose, the frog hopped downstairs and went back to the well.

'At last he is gone,' thought the relieved princess, 'and I shall hear from him no more.'

But the next evening as she was sitting down to dinner, the young princess again heard a gentle knock at the door and a voice crying out:

'Open the door, youngest daughter,

Remember thy promise, by the water!

Open the door, princess dear!

Thy true love, awaits thee here!'

Reluctantly, the princess let the frog dine with her and let him sleep on her pillow.

But she was becoming used to him now, and didn't find him quite so disgusting. After all, he was a polite frog, with good manners and lovely kind eyes. Again at sunrise, the frog hopped downstairs back to the well, and the princess found she actually missed his company.

The princess was not surprised to hear another knock at the door on the third night and a voice crying out:

'Open the door, youngest daughter,

Remember thy promise, by the water!

Open the door, princess dear!

Thy true love, awaits thee here!'

Again she dined with the frog, this time quite happily. She cheerfully chatted with him as they ate and carried him up to her room where again he slept on her pillow.

Imagine her surprise the next morning as the sun was rising when she woke. The princess was astonished to see, instead of a frog, a handsome prince standing next to her bed looking down on her with kind and beautiful eyes.

The handsome prince told her that he had been cursed by an evil witch, who had changed him into a frog. He was destined to stay a frog forever, unless a beautiful princess would let him eat from her plate and sleep on her pillow for three nights in a row.

'You have broken the evil spell,' the handsome prince said. 'Come with me to my father's kingdom and marry me and I will love you as long as you live.'

The young princess was overjoyed and accepted his hand in marriage.

As they spoke together, a golden carriage drove up outside, pulled by eight powerful horses decked with feathers and a golden harness. Behind the coach was the prince's servant Faithful Henry, who had been so unhappy when his dear master had been turned into a frog by the witch that his heart had nearly broken.

Faithful Henry helped the prince and princess into the carriage and drove them to the prince's kingdom.

As they drove away, they heard the sound of Faithful Henry singing at the top of his voice, so overjoyed was he that his master was free and happy. When they reached the kingdom, the prince and the princess were married and lived happily ever after.

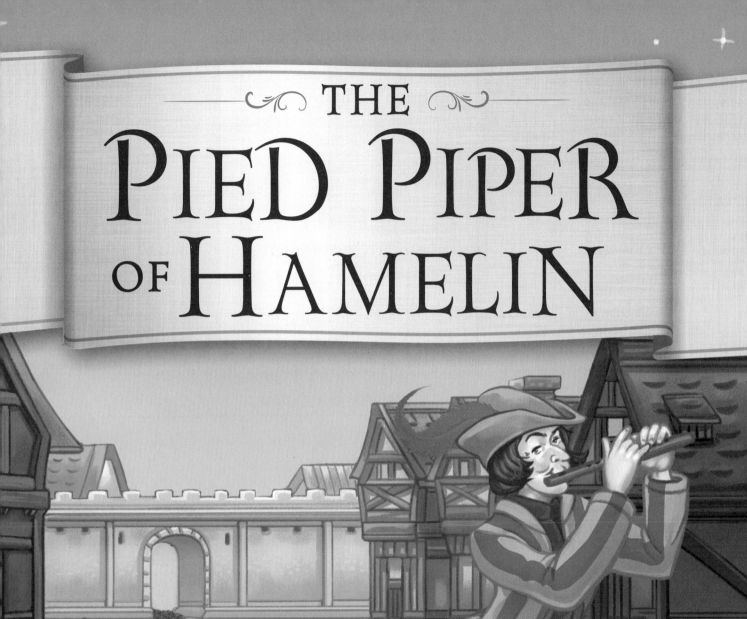

THE
PIED PIPER
OF HAMELIN

In the year 1284, the town of Hamelin in Germany became overrun by bands of rats, the likes of which had never been seen before or will be seen again.

These were no ordinary rats. They were huge black creatures that boldly ran down the street in broad daylight. They swarmed in the houses so much that the poor townspeople could not put their hands or their feet down anywhere without touching one.

When the townspeople dressed in the morning, they would find rats in their breeches and petticoats, in their pockets and in their boots. When they wanted something to eat, the people would find that the rats had eaten everything in the house.

It was even worse at night time. When they lay down to sleep, the townspeople would find rats under the sheets. Once the lights were put out, the nibbling rats would set to work. Everywhere would be the noise of gnawing rats, chewing and crunching away on whatever they could find. In the ceilings, the floors, the walls, the cupboards and the cellars, the raucous noise of rats rummaging and giving chase was so great that even a deaf man could not have had a full hour's rest.

Try as they might, the townspeople of Hamelin could not get rid of the rats. Neither cats nor dogs, poisons nor traps, prayers nor candles could do anything about the plague. The more rats they killed, the more came.

One Friday in despair, the townspeople gathered outside the town hall and noisily demanded that the mayor and the town councillors do something about the rat problem. The town council assembled in the town hall to consider what they could do to combat the awful plague.

The crowd outside was waiting impatiently for a resolution from the council when they noticed a strange-looking man walking into the square. He had an odd face, with a large crooked nose and piercing but mocking blue eyes. However, he had an easy smile on his lips.

The man was wearing a large felt hat with a scarlet rooster's feather set in it and was dressed in a long red and yellow jacket with a leather belt and green breeches. He was tall and thin and was carrying a wooden pipe. As he entered the town square, he was singing:

'Who lives shall see,

This is he,

The ratcatcher.'

When he stopped singing, the stranger asked the townspeople to send word to the town council and the mayor that, if they would make it worth his while, he would rid them of every single rat in the town before nightfall.

On hearing this message, the town council and the mayor brought the strange piper before them to discuss his proposal.

'Please Your Honours,' said the piper, 'I am able to draw all creatures living under the sun after me by means of a secret charm. I've helped other towns by using this charm on all sorts of creatures that cause ill. People call me the Pied Piper.'

'He must be a sorcerer!' exclaimed one man. 'We must beware of him!'

'I am just a poor piper,' replied the stranger. 'I've used my pipe to free a town from a huge swarm of mosquitoes. Another town was plagued with a brood of huge bats that filled the sky each night. I can rid your town of its rat infestation, if you will pay me a florin a head for each rat I kill.'

The council members and town citizens all gasped at this price.

'A florin a head!' exclaimed one councillor. 'But that will come to thousands of florins!'

The mayor looked around the council room. It was filled with the people of the town, waiting to hear his decision. But it was also filled with rats, which crawled over the desks, across the floor and around people's feet.

The mayor shrugged his shoulders and said to the stranger, 'A bargain! To work; we will pay you one florin a head, as you have requested.'

The piper announced he would start that very evening once the moon had risen. He told the townspeople that they should leave the streets free and content themselves with looking out their windows at what was passing, and that it would be an amazing spectacle. Then the piper left the town hall and the townspeople to their meeting.

The townspeople began to mutter among themselves, 'A florin a head! But this will cost us all a great deal of money!'

'Leave it to me,' said the mayor with a nasty smile.

The townspeople all nodded and laughed to each other, saying 'Leave it to the mayor.'

Towards nine o'clock that night, the Pied Piper stepped into the town square. The townspeople were all inside, as instructed, watching through their windows. As the moon rose, the piper gave a small smile and then raised his pipe to his lips. His eyes twinkling, he began to play on his pipe.

At first, he played three short, shrill notes over and over. But then, like a flame spreading from a small candle, the music grew and spread. It first grew into a slow caressing sound. Then it became more lively and urgent. Finally it built into a booming, piercing sound that spread through all the houses, alleyways, cellars, attics and secret places of the town.

As the townspeople listened to the music, they heard another sound begin to grow. It was an urgent rumbling noise. Then the townspeople realised it was the sound of the rats.

All of a sudden, thousands of rats burst out into the street and ran towards the piper. They flung themselves out from the cellars and the garrets, from under the furniture and from every nook and cranny of every house and building in the town. They filled the streets like a torrent of water, falling over each other and tumbling their way towards the town square and the piper.

Soon the piper was surrounded by thousands of rats. None came too close to him, but they all sat listening to the music, their noses twitching and their tails cocked.

Once the square was full, the piper turned around and, still playing, made his way down the street towards the River Weser, which ran along the walls of the town. As he walked and played, the rats all followed him closely, transfixed by the music.

When the piper arrived at the river he stopped walking but continued his piping. When the rats came to the river, they plunged into the whirling water and disappeared. For three hours, the piper played while rats flung themselves into the water and perished.

At last, at midnight, the very last rat made its way to the river. It was a big old, grey rat: the king of the band.

'Is that all of you?' the piper said to the rat king.

'That is all,' replied the rat king.

'How many of you are there?' asked the piper.

'We are nine hundred and ninety-nine thousand, nine hundred and ninety-nine,' replied the king.

'Thanks and go join them,' said the piper, and the old rat jumped into the river and disappeared beneath the surface.

When all the rats had gone, the townspeople ran into the street and joyfully celebrated. They rang the bells of the churches and sang and danced. Then they went to bed and, for the first time in many months, slept uninterrupted through the night.

The next morning, the Pied Piper made his way to the town hall, where the town council and the mayor were waiting for him. A great number of townspeople had also come to see the proceedings.

'Good morning sirs,' said the piper to the councillors. 'All your rats took a jump in the river last night and not one of them will come back, I guarantee. There were nine hundred and ninety-nine thousand, nine hundred and ninety-nine, at one florin a head. It is time to give me my payment.'

The mayor leaned forward in his seat and nodded. 'Very well. Let us see the rats' heads and we shall pay you.'

The piper did not expect this treachery. He paled angrily and his eyes flashed. 'If you care to find the heads, then go and look in the river!' he exclaimed. 'That was not the nature of our agreement and you know it!'

'It is you who is not holding to our agreement,' replied the mayor, and he laughed cruelly. The town council and the townspeople laughed along with him at the piper's misfortune.

'You have been of use to us,' said the mayor. 'Even though you won't give us the proof we need, we will not let you go empty-handed.' He offered the piper fifty pieces of copper for his trouble.

'Keep your copper,' replied the piper. 'Those who cheat me will find that I can use my pipe in other ways.'

'Bah, do you think we care what a crooked piper can do?' laughed the mayor, and the townspeople jeered along with him. 'Do your worst! We're not scared of you!'

The piper pulled his hat over his eyes and went into the street. The townspeople rubbed their hands together when they heard how they had avoided paying the piper and laughed at his misfortune.

The next day was Sunday and all the adults of the town went off merrily to church, thinking that at last they would be able to enjoy a Sunday lunch without the rats' interference. But they never suspected what terrible thing awaited them when they returned home.

All the children of the town had disappeared. Soon a terrible cry went up in the town. 'Our children! Where are our poor children?' was the lament heard in every street.

Then through the east gate of the town came one small boy. He was lame and hobbled along, leaning on a crutch.

This is what the little lame boy told them:

While all the parents were off at church, the children heard a wonderful music sounding. At first it sounded like three short, sweet notes and then it built up into a wonderful merry tune. All the children of the town ran out into the streets, their small feet pattering and their hands clapping in joy. They danced and skipped to the town square, where they found the piper playing his pipe.

Then the piper began to walk and the children followed, dancing and singing, their hearts filled with delight. They made their way to the foot of the mountain near the town. As they approached, a wondrous portal opened wide in the side of the mountain. A great golden light shone out from the door. The piper made his way in and the children followed. When all were inside, the great door shut fast behind them.

All, save the little lame boy, who could not keep up with the dance and lagged behind. The lame boy was terribly sad he'd been left behind and told the townspeople of the amazing sights the piper told the children they would see. He had promised the children a land of magic creatures, amazing fruits and bright birds.

The parents ran to the mountain and searched for the door, but were unable to find it. They returned desolate to the town, angry with the mayor and with themselves for cheating the piper out of what they had promised him. As the years passed, the townspeople of Hamelin became known for their kindness to strangers and their fairness to merchants and traders who passed through.

The children were never seen again, although many years later, the people heard stories of a place in a country called Transylvania where the people only spoke German but did not know how they came to be there. It was always thought, while hard to believe, these people must be the descendants of the children of Hamelin. For surely there are more difficult things in the world to believe than that.

HANSEL
AND
GRETEL

Once upon a time on the outskirts of a great forest there dwelt a poor woodcutter with his wife and his two children. The boy was called Hansel and the girl was called Gretel. The family was very poor and struggled to find enough to live on. Then one day a great famine fell upon the land and the woodcutter was unable to provide them with even their daily bread.

One night as the woodcutter lay in bed, tossing and turning with anxiety, he turned to his wife and said, 'What is to become of us? How are we to feed our poor children when we don't even have enough for ourselves?'

'I'll tell you what, husband,' answered the woman. 'Early tomorrow morning we shall take the children into the thickest part of the forest. We shall light a fire for them and give them each one more piece of bread. Then we'll go off to our work and leave them alone. They won't be able to find their way home through the forest and we shall be rid of them.'

'No, wife,' said the man. 'I will not do that. How could I stand to abandon my children alone in the forest? Wild animals would soon find them and devour them!'

'Oh, you fool!' said the woman. 'Then all four of us will starve together! You may as well prepare our coffins now!' And she gave him no peace until he agreed.

'But I do feel sorry for the poor children,' said the man.

The two children had been lying awake, unable to sleep because they were hungry, so they heard what their stepmother said to their father.

Gretel began to cry bitterly, as she thought they were doomed. 'Don't cry Gretel,' said Hansel, 'and do not worry. I will soon find a way to help us.'

When the adults had fallen asleep, Hansel got out of bed and put on his coat. He opened the door and crept outside. The moon was shining brightly and the white pebbles that lay in front of the house gleamed like silver coins. Hansel bent down and collected the pebbles until his pockets were stuffed full.

Hansel went back inside and said to Gretel, 'Don't worry, little sister. Sleep in peace and all will be well.'

Before daybreak, the woman roused the children, saying, 'Get out of bed, you sluggards! We're going into the forest to fetch some wood!' She gave them both a piece of bread for their dinner, telling them not to eat it before then, for they would get nothing else.

Gretel took the bread under her apron, as Hansel's pockets were full of the pebbles. Then they all set out into the forest.

After they had gone a little way, the man noticed that Hansel kept turning and looking back at the cottage. 'Hansel, why do you keep looking back and lagging behind?' he said. 'Pay attention and don't forget how to use your legs!'

'Ah, father,' Hansel replied, 'I am looking at my little white cat. It is sitting on the roof and wants to say goodbye to me.'

'You fool, that isn't your cat!' said the woman. 'That is just the morning sun shining on the chimney!'

However, Hansel had not been looking back for his cat. Instead, he'd been dropping the white pebbles on to the path.

They reached the middle of the forest and the father said, 'Pile up some wood, children, and I will make a fire so you won't be cold.'

Hansel and Gretel gathered some wood and the man lit the fire. When the flames were high, the woman said, 'Now children, lie down beside the fire and rest while we go into the forest to cut some wood. We will come back and fetch you when we are done.'

Hansel and Gretel sat by the fire and waited. When midday passed, they each ate their little piece of bread. They thought their father was still nearby, as they heard what sounded like the strokes of an axe. However, it was a branch that the woodcutter had set up so that when the wind blew, it knocked against a tree. Finally the children fell asleep by the fire.

It was night when they woke up. Gretel began to cry, but Hansel said, 'Wait a little until the moon comes up and then we will find the way.'

When the full moon rose, Hansel took Gretel by the hand. They followed the pebbles, which shone like newly minted coins, showing the way.

They walked all night through the forest. As dawn was breaking, they arrived back at the woodcutter's cottage. They knocked on the door and the woman opened it. When she saw Hansel and Gretel, she exclaimed, 'You naughty children! Why have you slept so long in the forest? We thought you were never coming back at all!'

Their father, however, was overjoyed, for he had not wanted to leave them in the forest alone.

Not long afterward, the famine struck again and one evening the children heard the woman saying to their father, 'We have eaten everything we have again. We only have half a loaf of bread and then that is it. Let's take the children deeper into the forest and leave them there. They won't be able to find their way out this time. There's no other way of saving ourselves!'

The man was very disheartened and said, 'Would it not be better to share our last bit with the children?' But the woman would not listen and scolded him. Because he had given in the first time, he had to give in the second time.

When the adults were asleep, Hansel got up and went to the door to gather more pebbles. However the woman had locked the door and he could not get out. But he comforted his sister and said, 'Sleep well little sister. We will find a way.'

Early next morning, the woman roused the children from their beds. She gave them a piece of bread, even smaller than the last time. As they headed into the woods, Hansel crumbled the bread in his pocket and stopped every now and then to throw some crumbs to the ground.

'Hansel! Why are you stopping and looking around?' asked the man. 'Keep walking straight ahead!'

'I am looking back at my little pigeon,' Hansel replied. 'It is sitting on the roof and it wants to say goodbye to me.'

'Foolish boy!' said the woman. 'That is not your pigeon! It is the morning sun shining on the chimney.' Hansel, however, little by little, threw all his crumbs on the path.

The woman took the children deep into the forest to a part that they had never been to before. As before, they made a fire. 'We are going to cut more wood,' said the woman. 'Stay by the fire and we will return to collect you in the evening when we are done.'

At midday, Gretel shared her piece of bread with Hansel, as he had scattered his along the path. Then they fell asleep and did not awake until it was dark. Hansel comforted his sister and said, 'Just wait until the moon rises and we shall see the breadcrumbs I have scattered. They will lead us back home.'

The moon rose and they set out, but the children could not find any crumbs. The birds of the woods had eaten them all. 'We shall soon find the way,' Hansel said to Gretel, but they could not find it.

They walked the whole night and all the next day from morning to evening but they could not get out of the forest. The children were very hungry, as they had only eaten two or three berries, which they found on the ground. They grew so weary that their legs could not carry them, so they lay under a tree and fell asleep.

It was now three mornings since they had left their father's cottage. They began to walk again but they were still deep in the forest and if help did not come soon they would die from weariness and hunger.

When it was midday, they saw a beautiful snow-white bird sitting in a tree. It sang so beautifully that they stopped to listen. When it stopped singing, it flew away in front of them and they followed it until they reached a little house.

Hansel and Gretel approached the house and saw that it was made of gingerbread with a roof covered with cakes. The windows were made of clear sugar.

'We will set to work on that and have a good meal!' exclaimed Hansel. He reached up and broke a piece off the roof while Gretel leant against the window and nibbled at the panes.

As they were eating, the children heard a soft voice calling out from the inside of the house:

'Nibble, nibble little mouse,

Who is nibbling at my house?'

The children answered:

'The wind, the wind,

The heaven-born wind!'

The children continued to eat, without being distracted. Hansel tore a great piece off the roof, as he very much liked the taste, and Gretel pushed out a whole window pane and sat down to eat it.

Suddenly the door opened and a very old woman bent over a walking stick came creeping out. Hansel and Gretel were terribly frightened and dropped what they were holding.

The old woman, however, nodded to them and said, 'Oh you poor children, what has brought you here? Come in and stay with me. No harm shall come to you.'

She took them by the hand and led them into the house, where she made them a good meal of milk and pancakes with sugar and apples and nuts. After this, she showed them to two pretty beds covered with clean white linen. Hansel and Gretel lay down in them and thought they must be in heaven.

Alas, the old woman had only pretended to be kind. She was really a wicked witch who lay in wait for children. She had made her sweet little house in order to entice them to her. If she captured a child, she would cook it and eat it and have a large feast.

Witches have red eyes that cannot see very far but they have a sense of smell like a bloodhound and are aware when people are near. When Hansel and Gretel had come near, the witch had laughed wickedly and said, 'Now I have them! They shall not escape!'

Early in the morning before the children awoke, the witch looked at them lying asleep so peacefully with their pretty, plump, rosy cheeks and she muttered, 'They will make a pretty mouthful!' The witch seized Hansel with her withered hand and carried him out to a little stall and locked him behind a cage door. He cried out but there was no one to help him.

Then the witch woke Gretel and cried out, 'Get up, lazy thing! Fetch some water and cook something for your brother. He is locked in the stall and is to be fattened up! When he is fat enough, I shall eat him!' Gretel began to cry bitterly, but it was in vain and she was forced to do as the witch commanded.

Hansel was given the best food to eat every day, but Gretel got nothing but crab shells. Every morning the witch went to Hansel and cried out, 'Stretch out your finger so I may feel if you are fat yet!'

However, Hansel had found a small bone which he stretched out to her, and the old witch, who had dim eyes, thought it was his finger and was astonished that he was still not fattening up.

Four weeks passed by and the witch grew impatient that Hansel was not getting fatter. Deciding she could wait no longer, the witch shouted out, 'Gretel! Bring me some water! Whether Hansel is fat or lean, tomorrow I will cook him up and eat him!'

How Gretel cried when she heard this. 'Keep your noise to yourself!' scolded the witch. 'It won't help!'

Early the next morning Gretel had to go outside and hang the cauldron filled with water and light the fire. 'We will bake first,' said the witch. 'I have heated the oven and kneaded the dough already.'

She pushed Gretel out to the oven, from which fiery flames were already darting. 'Creep inside,' the witch said, 'and see if it is warm enough, so we can put the bread in.' Once Gretel was inside, she intended to shut the door and bake her and eat her too.

However, Gretel saw what the witch intended and said, 'I do not know how I am to do it. How am I to get in?'

'You silly goose!' said the old witch. 'The door is big enough for you. Look, I can get in myself,' and she thrust her head in the oven. Then Gretel gave her a push that sent the witch right into the oven, and then she shut the iron door and bolted it.

How the witch yelled, but Gretel ran away and left the witch to her fate.

Gretel ran to Hansel and opened his cage door. 'Hansel, we are saved!' she cried. 'The old witch is dead!'

Hansel sprang from the cage like a bird and the children embraced and rejoiced. They went into the witch's house and found chests full of pearls and jewels.

'These are better than pebbles!' said Hansel and he filled his pockets with them.

Gretel said, 'I too will take some home,' and she filled her apron.

'Now we must get out of this witch's forest,' said Hansel.

They walked for several hours until they came to a great, wide lake. 'We cannot cross,' said Hansel. 'There's no ford or bridge.'

'And no ferry,' added Gretel, 'but look, there is a white duck swimming over there. Maybe she will help us.' Then she cried:

'Little duck, little duck, dost thou see,
Hansel and Gretel are waiting for thee?
There's not a plank or bridge in sight,
Take us across on thy back so white.'

The duck swam over and Hansel climbed on its back and told his sister to sit by him. 'No,' Gretel replied. 'We shall be too heavy together. She shall take us across one after the other.'

The good duck did so and when the children were on the other side and had walked a short while, they realised that the forest seemed more familiar to them.

Hansel and Gretel walked further until they saw their father's house. They ran to the house, rushed in and threw their arms around the woodcutter's neck.

Their father had not known a moment of happiness since he had left the children in the forest, but the woman, however, had died. Gretel emptied her apron until jewels spilled across the floor and Hansel pulled handful after handful of precious stones out of his pockets. Then all their troubles and cares were at an end and they lived together in perfect happiness.

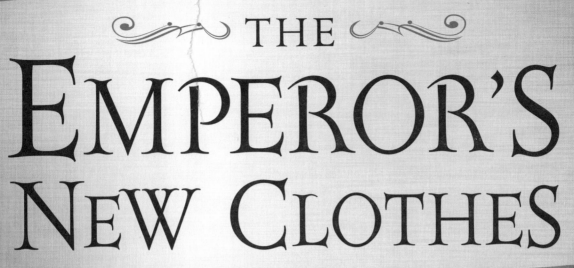

THE
EMPEROR'S
NEW CLOTHES

Many years ago, there lived an emperor who was so fond of fine clothes that he spent all his money on his outfits. He was so vain that he didn't care about his soldiers or going to the theatre or hunting; all he cared about was how well dressed he was. Whenever he went out, it was so he could show off his clothes. The emperor had a different suit for every hour of the day. Where most rulers could be found in their court with their ministers, the emperor could always be found in his wardrobe.

The great city where the emperor ruled was very merry and busy, and many travellers, merchants and strangers from far away travelled to visit and do business there.

One day, two tricksters arrived in town, claiming that they were weavers of the finest cloth. They told everyone that they could weave luxurious material of the most beautiful colours and elaborate patterns. The clothes that were made from this material, they claimed, had the amazing property of remaining invisible to anyone who was unfit for the position they held or who was incredibly simple.

'What marvellous cloth that must be!' thought the emperor when he heard about it. 'If I had clothes made from that material, I could tell who is unfit for their positions! I'd also be able to see who is wise and who is foolish. I must get this cloth woven for me straight away!'

The emperor summoned the two swindlers and gave them their instructions for his suit. He gave them large sums of money so they could start work immediately. The weavers set up two enormous looms in a comfortable room where they could work and sleep.

To make the cloth, the weavers asked for the most delicate silk and for thread made out of pure gold. They sat in front of the empty looms all day and into the night pretending to weave, but they really stowed the expensive silk and thread in their packs so they could sell it later.

After some time had passed, the emperor thought to himself, 'I should very much like to see how the weavers are getting on with the cloth.'

But when he remembered that someone who was unfit for his position or who was extremely simple could not see the cloth, the emperor became uneasy about going to see for himself. Indeed, everyone in the town knew about the amazing properties of the cloth and was eagerly looking forward to discover who of their friends and neighbours could not see it.

'I am sure that there is nothing for me to fear, really,' thought the emperor after some deliberation, 'but it might be best to send someone else first to let me know how it is going before I trouble myself. I will send my honest old minister to the weavers. He will be the best judge of how it looks, as he is a man of sense, and no one is more suited for their position than he is.'

The faithful old minister went along to the weavers' rooms, where the two swindlers were pretending to work with all their might at their empty looms.

'What can this mean?' thought the minister, his eyes opening wide. 'I cannot see anything at all!'

The two imposters invited him to come near and look at the cloth. They asked the minister if the design pleased him and if he thought that the colours were very beautiful, pointing at their empty looms all the while. The poor minister tried his very best to see the cloth, but he couldn't see anything, simply because there was nothing to be seen.

'Oh dear,' thought the minister. 'Could it be that I am a simpleton? I have never thought so, but if I am, no one must know. Maybe I am not fit for my position? No, that must not be discovered either. I mustn't say that I can't see the cloth.'

'Now, dear minister, what do you think? Does our work please you?' asked one of the swindlers, still pretending to work at the loom.

'Oh it is excellent!' replied the minister. 'It is exceedingly beautiful! What stunning colours! What brilliant patterns! I shall tell the emperor that I like the cloth very much.'

'We are very pleased to hear that,' said the rogues, and they proceeded to explain the pattern and to describe the beautiful colours.

The minister then explained it all to the emperor. The weavers then asked for more silk and gold so they could finish what they'd begun. However, everything they received was stowed in their packs to be sold later and they continued to work away at the empty looms.

Soon afterwards, the emperor decided to send another trusted member of his court to the weavers to see how they were progressing and if the cloth was nearly finished. Like the old minister, the courtier looked and looked, but couldn't see anything, as there was nothing to be seen.

'It is a beautiful piece of cloth, is it not?' asked the two tricksters, showing and describing the magnificent colours and patterns, which did not really exist.

'I am not stupid,' thought the courtier in a panic, 'so I must not be fit for my position. I must not let anyone know this is the case!'

So the courtier praised the cloth, which he couldn't see.

'It is indeed extraordinarily magnificent, Your Imperial Majesty,' said the courtier to the emperor when he returned to make his report.

By now, everyone in the town was talking about the incredible cloth. The emperor decided that he must go and see it for himself, while it was still on the loom. Accompanied by a number of officials, including the two who had already visited the weavers, he went to see the progress of the cloth. When they saw the emperor approaching, the two rogues pretended to work harder than ever, although they still didn't pass any thread through the loom.

'Is it not magnificent?' said the two officials who had already been there before. 'Your Majesty must admire the colours and patterns.'

They pointed to the empty looms, as they imagined that the others must be able to see the cloth and did not want them to know that they could not.

'What is this?' thought the emperor in dismay. 'I do not see anything at all! Am I stupid? Am I unfit for my position as emperor? That would be the worst thing imaginable!'

'Oh, the cloth is charming,' the emperor said aloud. 'It has my complete approval.'

He smiled and nodded as he looked at the empty loom, for he did not want to say that he could not see anything. All the officials with him looked and looked, and although they could not see anything, they all nodded and exclaimed, 'Magnificent! Beautiful!'

They advised the emperor to have some clothes made from the cloth for a great procession that was soon to take place. Everyone seemed to be delighted and the emperor even presented the weavers with ribbons of knighthood and the titles Imperial Court Weavers.

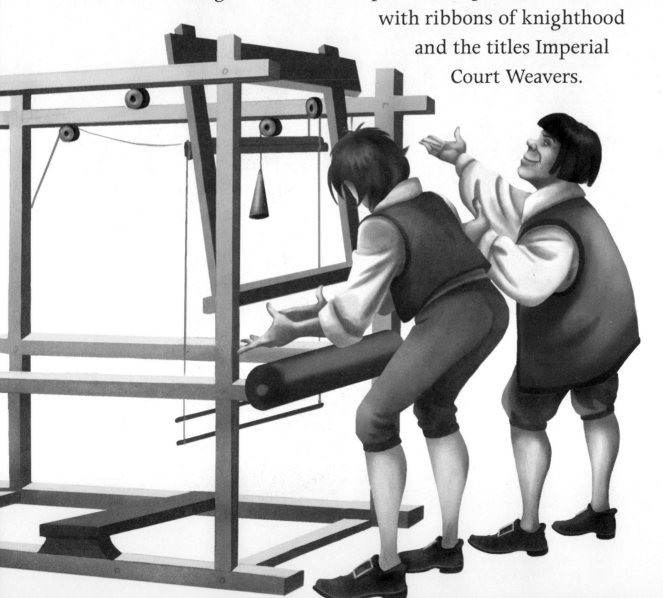

The day before the procession, the tricksters pretended to work on the Emperor's outfit. They pretended to take the cloth from the loom and cut in the air with big scissors. They acted at sewing the invisible cloth with needles. At last, they announced, 'The emperor's new suit is ready!'

The emperor came to the weavers with all the officials of his court to see the new clothes. The tricksters raised up their arms, as if they had a suit of clothing draped over them.

'Here are the trousers!' they said. 'This is the coat and this is the cloak! The cloth is as light as a cobweb. You might almost imagine you have nothing on when you are wearing it, but that is one of the virtues of this delicate cloth.'

'Indeed!' said all the court officials, even though they could not see anything.

'If Your Majesty will remove his clothes,' said the weavers, 'we will fit the new suit, in front of the mirror here.'

The emperor undressed and the swindlers pretended to dress him in the new suit. The emperor turned from side to side in front of the mirror, so he looked like he was admiring his new clothes.

'How wonderful His Majesty looks in his new suit and how well it fits!' everyone exclaimed. 'What a beautiful pattern! What fine colours!'

The master of ceremonies announced that the procession was about to start. 'I am ready,' said the emperor. 'Do my new clothes fit well?'

The courtiers who were to carry the royal train felt around on the ground, as though they were lifting the end of a cloak. They did not want people to think that they were simple or unfit for their position.

The emperor marched out in the middle of the procession under a beautiful canopy. All the townspeople were standing along the street and hanging out of the windows, waiting to see the new suit.

Everyone who saw him exclaimed, 'How magnificent are our emperor's new clothes! How well they fit him!'

No one wanted to admit that they could not see the outfit, because they didn't want their friends and neighbours to think that they were stupid or unfit for their positions.

As the emperor entered the great square there was a great roar. But in the moment of quiet that followed the cheers, the voice of a little boy could be heard.

'But he has nothing on!' exclaimed the little boy.

'Good heavens! Listen to the voice of an innocent child!' exclaimed someone, and then the whole crowd started to whisper to each other, 'He has nothing on!'

The voices got louder until everyone was shouting, 'He has nothing on!' at the tops of their voices and roaring with laughter.

The emperor tried for a moment or two to remain dignified, then took to his heels and scurried back to the palace. The two tricksters had fled, taking all their gold and precious silk with them, and were never seen again.

And from that time on, the emperor became less vain about his clothes.

CINDERELLA

Once upon a time there lived a gentleman with his young daughter. His wife had passed away, but their daughter had inherited her mother's rare goodness and sweetness of temper.

After several years had passed, the gentleman decided to marry again. Unhappily, his choice of bride was a poor one, for the lady he married was the proudest and most haughty woman imaginable. She had two daughters of her own, who were like her in every way.

The wedding was barely over when the woman's temper began to show. She could not bear the sweetness of the young girl, as it made her own daughters seem even worse. The stepmother gave her the dirtiest, hardest work in the house to do. Every day, she had to scour the dishes, clean the tables, polish the grates, scrub the floors and dust the bedrooms.

The poor girl was forced to sleep in the cold, bare attic on a pile of straw, while her two stepsisters slept in luxurious beds in fine bedrooms lined with mirrors so they could see their fine clothes. The young girl only had a plain shabby cotton dress to wear.

The girl bore all this patiently and did not even complain to her father, who was completely ruled by his wife, as she did not wish to add to his unhappiness. When her work was done, she would sit in the corner next to the chimney among the cinders. Her stepsisters mocked her and called her 'Cinderella'. However, despite her poor clothes and her daily toil, Cinderella was a hundred times more lovely than her stepsisters, despite their fine clothes.

It came to pass that the king's son came of age. A grand ball was announced in his honour and the most important and fashionable people in the town were invited. When their invitation arrived, the stepsisters immediately busied themselves with choosing their gowns, petticoats and jewellery for the occasion. Poor Cinderella spent her days lacing corsets, ironing dresses, picking up discarded clothes, sewing and shopping. The sisters instructed her to style their hair and paint their faces in different ways to see what looked best.

On the night of the ball, Cinderella busily dressed the stepsisters. They taunted her, saying, 'Cinderella, don't you wish that you were going to the ball?'

'Ah, you are laughing at me,' Cinderella sighed. 'It is not for such as I to think about going to balls.'

'You are right,' the stepsisters replied. 'How people would laugh to see a cinder wench dancing at a ball!'

With that, the two stepsisters climbed into their fine carriage and drove off to the ball. Cinderella watched until they were out of sight, and then sat in her corner next to the chimney and burst into tears.

Suddenly a kindly little old lady appeared out of nowhere in front of Cinderella, who was so startled that she stopped crying.

'Dear Cinderella, I am your godmother,' said the woman, who was a fairy. 'Why are you crying? Is it because you wish you could go to the ball?'

'Yes, indeed Godmother!' exclaimed Cinderella.

'Well, do what I say and I shall send you there,' said the fairy godmother. 'But first, I must get you ready. Run to the garden and fetch me a pumpkin.'

Cinderella ran out the kitchen door and soon came back with the largest pumpkin she could find. Her fairy godmother laid it on the ground and tapped it with her wand. The simple pumpkin turned into a beautiful coach made of the finest gold.

Next, the fairy godmother looked in the mousetrap in the pantry and saw that six mice were caught there, poking their noses through the bars. As she freed each mouse, the fairy tapped it with her wand. Each mouse turned into a handsome coach horse, with an elegant long neck, a sweeping tail and a lovely mouse-grey coat.

Then the fairy directed Cinderella to the garden, where she found six lizards. They were soon transformed into six footmen, all wearing shining green and silver coats.

Finally, Cinderella was sent to look in the rat trap. She returned with a great rat with a long beard. One wave of the fairy godmother's wand and the rat turned into a jolly coachman with the finest whiskers imaginable.

'Well my dear, is this equipage fit for the ball?' asked the fairy godmother.

'Why yes!' exclaimed Cinderella. Then she paused and looked down at her shabby, dirty dress. 'But must I go as I am, wearing these rags?'

The fairy godmother touched Cinderella with her wand. Cinderella's shabby dress changed into a beautiful ball gown of gold and silver that sparkled with diamonds. On her feet she wore dainty slippers made of perfect glass.

'Now, my dear, you can go to the ball,' said the fairy godmother. 'Just remember one thing. You must leave before the clock strikes midnight, otherwise your dress will become rags again, your carriage a pumpkin, your horses mice, your footmen lizards and your coachman a rat.'

Cinderella promised she would leave before midnight and then climbed into her coach and drove away, her heart full of joy.

When she arrived at the ball, the whole palace was struck with how beautiful she was. As soon as he saw her, the prince was in love. He came forward and lead her into the ballroom and begged her to dance with him the whole evening. Everyone marvelled at her elegance and grace as she danced and all the ladies admired Cinderella's fine gown and imagined how they could have a dress made just like it.

When supper was served, the prince waited on her himself and was so enamoured that he could not eat. Cinderella saw her stepsisters looking at her in admiration, but when she spoke to them, they did not recognise her. Time passed quickly and soon Cinderella heard the clock chiming eleven and three quarters. She quickly made her exit and returned home.

Cinderella told her fairy godmother about her lovely evening and how the prince had begged her to return for the second night of the ball. As she was talking, she heard her stepsisters return home and ran to meet them, rubbing her eyes as though she had been sleeping.

'If you had been there, you would have seen such a sight!' exclaimed one sister. 'A beautiful princess attended. No one knows who she is but the prince is smitten and would give the world to know her name. How honoured we were when she spoke to us!'

'Oh I would so like to see her,' said Cinderella. 'Could you not lend me a dress so I could attend the ball, just to catch a glimpse?'

'Don't be ridiculous!' snapped the other sister. 'I would not be so silly as to lend my clothes to a cinder maid!' Cinderella was glad, as she had asked in jest and knew that she would be refused.

The next night, the two stepsisters attended the ball and so did Cinderella, dressed even more magnificently. The prince was constantly by her side and Cinderella so enjoyed his company that she did not notice how the time flew by.

Suddenly, Cinderella heard the clock start to strike twelve. She ran from the ballroom as fast as she could. The prince followed but he could not overtake her. As she ran, she left behind one of her glass slippers on the palace stairs. When Cinderella got home, her clothes had returned to rags but she was clutching the other glass slipper.

The stepsisters returned soon after and Cinderella asked them how they had enjoyed the ball and if the mysterious princess had attended. They replied that she had, but when the clock struck twelve, the princess had run from the ballroom in such haste that she had left behind one of her glass slippers. The prince had picked it up and spent the rest of the ball gazing at it, so in love was he.

A few days later, it was proclaimed that the prince would marry whoever could perfectly fit the glass slipper. All the ladies of the court and palace tried on the slipper, but none could fit into it. It was laid upon a silk cushion and taken to all the ladies of the town for them to try, but to no avail.

When it came to the house of the stepsisters, they tried all they could to fit their feet into the slipper. They pushed and shoved and curled their toes, but the slipper was too small and dainty for them.

'Let me try,' said Cinderella.

The two sisters laughed at her and began to tease her, but the courtier who had been sent with the slipper said that he had orders that every woman must try it on. He slipped the slipper on her foot and found that it fitted as perfectly as if it had been made for her.

As the astonished stepsisters looked on, the fairy godmother appeared and waved her wand and they saw before them the beautiful lady from the ball. They threw themselves before Cinderella and begged her to forgive them. Cinderella was so good that she bade them rise and embraced them.

Cinderella was taken to the prince. When he saw her, the prince thought Cinderella was more beautiful than ever and he fell to his knees and asked her to marry him. A few days later they were married and they lived happily ever after.

THE END

SLEEPING BEAUTY

Although earlier versions are thought to have influenced this tale, the first recorded version of *Sleeping Beauty* was written by Italian Giambattista Basile in 1636. His story, entitled *Sun, Moon and Talia*, is much longer than the story modern readers are familiar with.

Charles Perrault, the French fairytale collector, used Basile's version as the basis for his tale of 1697, the first to be titled *Sleeping Beauty*. The prince marries Sleeping Beauty and they have two children, but his mother, who is part ogre, disapproves. When he is away at war, the mother orders the cook to serve her the children and their mother to eat, but the cook hides them away and substitutes a lamb, a goat and a deer. The ogress discovers the hidden family and prepares a pit of snakes for them, but the king arrives home in time to save them. Instead, the ogress meets the fate she had reserved for Sleeping Beauty and her children.

Modern readers are most familiar with the Brothers Grimm version of *Sleeping Beauty*. Titled *Briar Rose*, this much milder tale ends with the marriage of Sleeping Beauty and the prince. It is also the first version to have the prince awaken her with a kiss.

THE UGLY DUCKLING

Danish author Hans Christian Andersen wrote *The Ugly Duckling* in 1843 and it was published in 1844 in his collection *Nye Eventyr* (*New Fairytales*). This story is one of his most popular and famous tales. Andersen quite openly admitted that *The Ugly Duckling* was autobiographical in nature and was a metaphor for his own life.

Andersen was the son of a shoemaker and a washerwoman. His father and grandmother believed that the family was descended from nobility, although this has never been proven. His father died when he was young and Andersen worked as an apprentice weaver and tailor. He moved to Copenhagen at the age of fourteen to work as an actor at the Royal Danish Theatre, where he worked until his voice broke. One of the theatre directors gave him a grant to attend school, which was one of the darkest periods of his life. Tormented by the headmaster, who tried to 'harden' his character, Andersen was several years older than the other students. He was often made fun of and was teased for his unattractive appearance, large nose and close-set eyes. Once Andersen left school, he attended university and started writing seriously, where he found success and became known for his fairytales.

Andersen was inspired to write *The Ugly Duckling* in 1842 while he was spending the summer at a manor house in the countryside that had swans living in the garden. The story was also known as *The Cygnet*. The collection was an immediate success, both among readers and critics. Many reviewers and scholars draw parallels between the hardships endured by the duckling and events in Andersen's childhood. When he was asked if he would one day write his autobiography, Andersen claimed that it had already been written in the form of *The Ugly Duckling*.

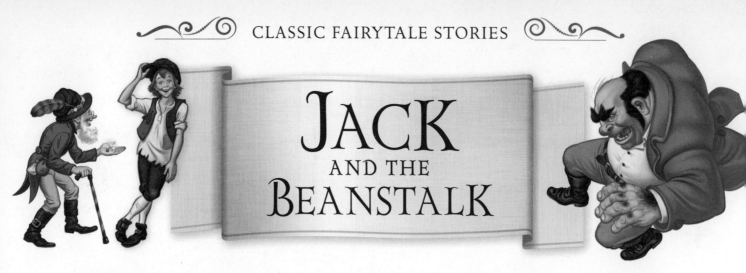

JACK
AND THE
BEANSTALK

The earliest known modern version of *Jack and the Beanstalk* was published in 1807 by Benjamin Talbert and republished by Andrew Lang in 1890 in *The Red Fairy Book*, although it is thought that earlier versions had been well known for several centuries. A comic play called *The Story of Jack Spriggins and the Enchanted Bean* was published in 1734. Joseph Jacob's 1890 publication of the story is the best-known, and is also thought to be closer to the original folk version. The Jacobs version is used in this collection.

The Talbert version of the story was a much more moralistic tale. The strange old man that Jack meets on the road has been sent by a fairy. When Jack climbs the beanstalk, the fairy meets him and tells him the tale of the castle, which used to belong to a brave knight and his family. A giant bribed a servant to let him in the castle and he killed the knight and his family while they slept; all except for the mother and her baby, who were visiting her old nurse. It turns out that the dead knight's wife is Jack's mother and the baby is Jack. Jack is tasked with winning back the castle and his possessions from the giant. Ultimately the evil giant is killed and Jack regains his inheritance.

Joseph Jacob's better-known version removes these elements, which in Talbert's version served to justify Jack's stealing, and replaces them with a cheekier Jack. The Jack-the-trickster character is common in folklore, appearing in stories such as *Jack the Giant Killer*, *Little Jack Horner* and *The Jack Tales*, a collection of stories that originated in the Appalachian mountains in the US in the 18th century but were based on earlier English folktales.

THE FROG PRINCE

The *Frog Prince* is thought to date back to the 14th century. Variations on the story can be found across Europe, from Scotland to Hungary, and tales of princes transformed into frogs are told in China, Korea, India and Sri Lanka. *The Frog Prince* is also known as *The Frog King* or *Iron Henry* (or *Heinrich*). The story was recorded by the Brothers Grimm under the title *The Frog King* in their *Household Tales* collection and is the first tale in the book.

Earlier variations on the tale, such as *The Tale of the Queen Who Sought a Drink From a Certain Well*, *The Paddo* and *The Well of the World's End*, have the frog requesting that his head be cut off by the heroine, only to turn into a prince. In the Grimms' version, the princess does not let the frog sleep on her pillow but angrily throws the frog against the wall, transforming him back into a prince.

In their introduction to the story, the Grimms recorded a version of the story that removed the golden ball but included the frog spending three nights to have the enchantment removed. When the story was translated into English by Edgar Taylor in 1823, he removed the rather violent act of the princess throwing the frog and used the ending from the variation.

It is not known exactly when the element of kissing the frog to transform him was first introduced, despite the fact that it is one of the best-known aspects of the story for modern readers.

THE PIED PIPER OF HAMELIN

The town of Hamelin (or Hameln, in German) is a real place, set on the banks of the river Weser in northern Germany. The story of the pied piper is dated back to an unknown event that occurred in the town in 1284. A stained glass window placed in the church around 1300 seems to be the earliest reference to the tale. It depicted the piper and several children but was destroyed in 1660. The event is also referred to by a note found in a 14th century manuscript, as well as an early entry from the town records.

Historians can only speculate what happened in Hamelin, but theories include the children leaving to join a settlement movement to Eastern Europe, a children's crusade or a plague, with the piper representing death.

The rats were not part of the original story but were added in the 1500s by Count Froben Christoph von Zimmern. Englishman Richard Rowland Verstegan also produced a version in 1605 that included the first description of the piper as 'pied' (patched in many colours). The Brothers Grimm published *The Children of Hameln* in their collection of folktales in 1816 and the English poet Robert Browning wrote a poem called *The Pied Piper of Hamelin: A Child's Story*, which became extremely popular and helped revive interest in the legend.

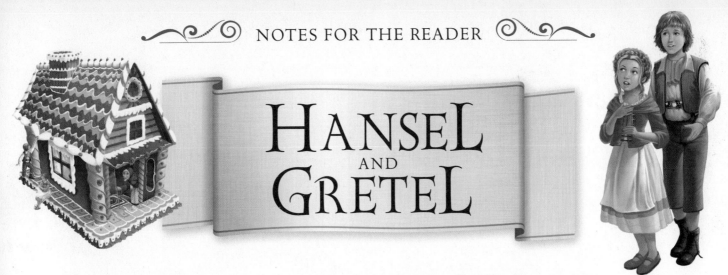

HANSEL AND GRETEL

Hansel and Gretel was originally recorded by the Brothers Grimm. They heard it from Dortchen Wild, a storyteller who later married Wilhelm Grimm.

The Grimms first recorded *Hansel and Gretel* in 1812, but there are differences between the original and the final edition of 1857. The most noticeable difference is the woman. In the original, she is the children's mother. By the final version, she was changed to a stepmother. This occurred in several fairytales (notably *Snow White*) to make the story appropriate for children and reflected the stories' popularity with the conservative middle class. Hansel and Gretel were named Little Brother and Little Sister. The Grimms chose the names Hansel and Gretel because they were so common; the German equivalents of John and Jane.

Stories about parents abandoning their children or children lost in the woods, such as *The Babes in the Wood* and *Baba Yaga*, are common across many cultures. In medieval times, it was not unknown for parents to abandon their children when they could no longer feed them. In their introduction, the Grimms note several stories with similar themes. In one, it is a wolf, not a witch, who lives in the house. In another, three princesses follow a thread, then a trail of ashes and finally peas, which are eaten by pigeons.

In 1893, *Hansel and Gretel* was turned into an opera by the German composer Engelbert Humperdinck. The opera became hugely popular and helped make the story as well-known as it is today.

THE EMPEROR'S NEW CLOTHES

Hans Christian Andersen included *The Emperor's New Clothes* in his collection of stories called *Fairy Tales, Told for Children*, published in 1837.

This story illustrates how well Andersen understands human behaviour. The emperor's pride and vanity end up causing his downfall. The insecurities and fears of everyone in the court and the town are exploited by the two swindlers, who realise that people will agree to almost anything to avoid being thought stupid or feeling excluded. It is only a child, who has not yet learnt to worry about the opinions of others, who can expose the fraud. This message about vanity, peer pressure and individuality still resonates today.

Although it is an original story, there are similar tales from different cultures across the ages about people being tricked through their own behaviour or stupidity. Other tales include a Sri Lankan king being tricked into wearing a silk robe that only well-born people can see, a Turkish king accepting a turban visible only to those born in wedlock, and various tales from the British Isles of wives convincing their husbands that they are dead, a watchdog or wearing clothes in a bid to see who has the stupidest spouse.

Andersen himself claims that the tale is of Spanish origin from the 13th century. His original version has the emperor continuing the procession even after his stupidity is revealed. 'I must carry on the procession until the end,' thinks the foolish emperor, as his courtiers continue to carry the imaginary train.

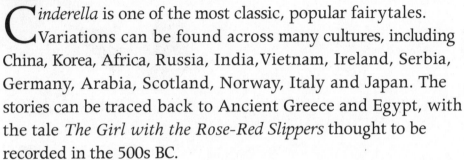

CINDERELLA

Cinderella is one of the most classic, popular fairytales. Variations can be found across many cultures, including China, Korea, Africa, Russia, India, Vietnam, Ireland, Serbia, Germany, Arabia, Scotland, Norway, Italy and Japan. The stories can be traced back to Ancient Greece and Egypt, with the tale *The Girl with the Rose-Red Slippers* thought to be recorded in the 500s BC.

The Grimm's version, *Aschenputtel* (*Ash Girl*), is about a girl who plants a hazel tree on her mother's grave that grants wishes. When she begs to go to the ball, her stepmother throws lentils into the ashes and tells her she may go if she picks them all out. Birds help pick out the lentils, but she is still not permitted to go. The tree grants her wish and she gets her dress. The third time she attends the ball, the prince smears the stairs with pitch to stop her. Her shoe is caught as she runs out. When the stepsisters try the shoe, the first cuts off her toe so the shoe fits, but is caught when blood seeps out. The second cuts off her heel but is also discovered. At the conclusion of the story, the birds peck out the stepsisters' eyes.

Modern readers are most familar with the version recorded by Frenchman Charles Perrault in his collection *Contes de ma Mere L'Oye* (*Tales of Mother Goose*). This story, called *Cendrillon*, was written in 1697 and saw the appearance of the fairy godmother, the pumpkin carriage and the glass slippers. Perrault's tale was written when fairytales were extremely popluar among the wealthy aristocracy and is much less violent than the Grimm's German version. The version in this collection is based on the Perrault tale.

ILLUSTRATORS

MIRELA TUFAN
Sleeping Beauty

OMAR ARANDA
The Ugly Duckling

The Emperor's New Clothes

ANTON PETROV
WATERMARK - AUCKLAND STUDIO

Jack and the Beanstalk

SUZIE BYRNE
MELISSA WEBB
The Frog Prince

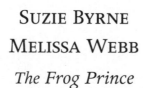

STEVIE MAHARDHIKA
WATERMARK - AUCKLAND STUDIO

The Pied Piper of Hamelin

BRIJBASI
Hansel and Gretel

MELISSA WEBB
Cinderella

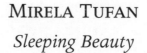